John Burningham
Mr Gumpy's Outing

and other stories

JONATHAN CAPE
London

The Rabbit
Mr Gumpy's Outing
Avocado Baby
The Shopping Basket
Borka
Courtney
Where's Julius?

This edition first published in the United Kingdom in 2000
by Jonathan Cape, The Random House Group Ltd,
20 Vauxhall Bridge Road, London SW1V 2SA

All seven titles first published by Jonathan Cape
The Rabbit © 1974 John Burningham
Mr Gumpy's Outing © 1970 John Burningham
The Shopping Basket © 1980 John Burningham
Borka © 1963 John Burningham
Courtney © 1994 John Burningham
Avocado Baby © 1982 John Burningham
Where's Julius? © 1986 John Burningham

ISBN 0224047582

Printed in Singapore by
Tien Wah Press(Pty) Ltd

The Rabbit

We have a rabbit

The rabbit has a hutch in the garden

His favourite food is dandelions

I like to stroke the rabbit

Sometimes the rabbit gets out

He likes to hop about in the garden

I would like him to stay in the garden
but he eats Daddy's plants

So I have to catch him

And put him back

Mr Gumpy's Outing

This is Mr Gumpy.

Mr Gumpy owned a boat and his house
was by a river.

One day Mr Gumpy went out in his boat.
  "May we come with you?" said the children.
  "Yes," said Mr Gumpy,
"if you don't squabble."

"Can I come along, Mr Gumpy?"
said the rabbit.
   "Yes, but don't hop about."

"I'd like a ride," said the cat.
    "Very well," said Mr Gumpy.
"But you're not to chase the rabbit."

"Will you take me with you?" said the dog.
"Yes," said Mr Gumpy.
"But don't tease the cat."

"May I come, please, Mr Gumpy?"
said the pig.
"Very well, but don't muck about."

23

"Have you got a place for me?" said the sheep.
"Yes, but don't keep bleating."

"Can we come too?" said the chickens.
"Yes, but don't flap," said Mr Gumpy.

"Can you make room for me?" said the calf.
"Yes, if you don't trample about."

"May I join you, Mr Gumpy?" said the goat.
"Very well, but don't kick."

For a while they all went along happily but then . . .

The goat kicked

The calf trampled

The chickens flapped

The sheep bleated

The pig mucked about

The dog teased the cat

The cat chased the rabbit

The rabbit hopped

The children squabbled

The boat tipped . . .

and into the water they fell.

Then Mr Gumpy and the goat and the calf
and the chickens and the sheep and the pig
and the dog and the cat and the rabbit and
the children all swam to the bank and
climbed out to dry in the hot sun.

"We'll walk home across the fields,"
said Mr Gumpy. "It's time for tea."

It was getting so strong it could

break out from the straps
on its high chair,

pull other children uphill in a cart,

wrench off the side of its cot.
  And each day Mrs Hargraves gave
the baby an avocado pear.

One night a burglar got into the house.

The baby woke up and, hearing the burglar moving about downstairs, leapt out of its cot.

The baby picked up a broom, and chased the burglar.

54

The burglar was so frightened at being chased by a baby that he dropped his bag and ran out of the house.

The next day Mr Hargraves put a notice on the gate. "That should keep the burglars away," he said.

The baby would help
carry the shopping,

move the furniture

and push the car
when it would
not start.

One day two bullies were waiting
for the children in the park.

The bullies started
being very nasty to
the children.

The baby did not like that
and jumped out of its push-chair,

picked up the bullies and

threw them into the pond.

The baby gets stonger every day and
of course it is still eating avocado pears.

Borka

The adventures
of a Goose
with no Feathers

Once upon a time there were two geese called Mr and Mrs Plumpster.

They lived on a deserted piece of marshland near the East Coast of England, where their ancestors had once lived many years before. There they built their nest and laid their eggs.

Each spring the Plumpsters came back to the marshes and mended their nest. Then Mrs Plumpster settled down to lay her eggs, and Mr Plumpster kept guard.

He hissed at anything that came near the nest.
   Sometimes he hissed even if there was nothing in sight.
It made him feel important.

Then the eggs began to hatch. One fine spring morning there were six baby Plumpsters in the nest.

Mr Plumpster was delighted, and he invited his friends round to celebrate.

The young geese were given names. They were:

Archie

Freda

Jennifer

Oswald

Timothy

and Borka

Now all the geese look very much alike when they are young, but right from the start there was something odd about Borka. Borka had a beak, wings and webbed feet like all her brothers and sisters, but she did not have any feathers.

Mr and Mrs Plumpster were very worried about this. They called the doctor goose who examined Borka carefully. He said there was nothing wrong with her except that she did not have any feathers. "A most unusual case," he went on, and he thought for a long while. Then he told Mrs Plumpster that there was only one thing to do. She must knit some feathers for Borka.

76

So Mrs Plumpster got out her knitting needles
and set to work. Of course she could not knit
real feathers, but she made a kind of grey
woollen jersey as much like feathers as she
could.

When she had finished, she called Borka
and tried it on her. Borka was delighted,
and flapped around with joy, because
she had always been chilly at night.

She went to show the other young geese, but they just laughed at her. This made her very unhappy and she went into a patch of tall reeds and cried.

Now by this time the other young geese were learning to fly and to swim properly. But Borka did not like joining in because the others teased her, and so she got very behind with her lessons.

Nobody noticed that she was not attending. Mr and Mrs Plumpster were far too busy. Borka did try to learn to swim, but whenever she went into the water, her jersey took such a long time to dry afterwards that she soon gave up.

By now the summer was almost over. The weather was getting cooler and the geese were becoming restless.

At this time of year they always went to a warmer land where it was easier to find food.

The Plumpsters began getting ready to leave. They covered their nest with twigs and rushes to keep it safe through the stormy winter.

Then one day it became really cold and wet.

The geese shivered, and knew it was time for them to go.

They chose one wise old goose to lead them and they all flew away.

But Borka did not go. She could not fly. Instead she went and hid, and watched them leave. Nobody noticed that she was missing. They were all too busy thinking of the journey ahead. As the geese disappeared into the grey sky, tears trickled down Borka's beak.

She did not know what to do.

It was drizzling, and she wandered off, hoping to find a
dry place for the night. It was already getting dark
when she came to a line of boats moored in the estuary.

Borka chose one that had no lights on board, and she walked up the gangplank.

She was just going down into the hold of the boat when
there was a loud bark. A dog came rushing out, which
gave Borka a terrible fright. But the dog, seeing it was
only a goose, stopped barking and introduced himself.
He was called Fowler.

Borka explained that she only wanted to stay under
cover for the night, so Fowler showed her into a part of
the hold where there were some old sacks for her to lie
on. She was so tired that she fell asleep almost at once.

Now the boat, which was called the *Crombie*, belonged to Captain McAllister. Late that night he and his mate, whose name was Fred, came back, and they decided to sail early in the morning before it was light. Fowler forgot all about Borka, who was still asleep in the hold.

It was not until they were well on their way that he
remembered, and told the Captain.
"Well, well!" said Captain McAllister.
"A goose on board! She'll have to work her passage if
she's coming with us to London."

Borka was soon very friendly with the Captain, Fred and, of course, with Fowler. She coiled pieces of rope with her beak, picked up crumbs from the floor and helped in any way she could.

In return she was given plenty of good food.

91

At last the *Crombie* steamed into the Thames and they were nearing London. Captain McAllister began to wonder what to do with Borka when they got there.

He decided to leave her in Kew Gardens, which is a large park where lots of geese live all the year round.

When they came to the place where the river flows past Kew Gardens, Captain McAllister lifted Borka over the railings and put her with the other geese. She was sorry to say goodbye to her friends but they promised to come and visit her on their next trip to London.

The geese at Kew did not mind that Borka had no feathers. There were already so many strange kinds of birds in the gardens. Nobody laughed at her grey woollen jersey and all the geese were very friendly, especially one called Ferdinand. Ferdinand cared for Borka and taught her to swim really well. She is still living there happily and whenever Captain McAllister and Fred and Fowler come to London they call in to see her.

So if you are in Kew Gardens at any time and you see a goose who looks somehow different from the others – it might well be Borka.

The Shopping Basket

"Pop down to the shop for me, will you, Steven, and buy six eggs, five bananas, four apples, three oranges for the baby, two doughnuts and a packet of crisps for your tea. And leave this note at number 25."

So Steven set off for the shop, carrying his basket. He passed number 25,

the gap in the railings,

the full litter basket,

the men digging up the pavement

and the house where the nasty dog lived,

and arrived at the shop.

He bought the six eggs, five bananas, four apples, three oranges for the baby, two doughnuts and a packet of crisps for his tea.

But when he came out of the shop there was a bear.

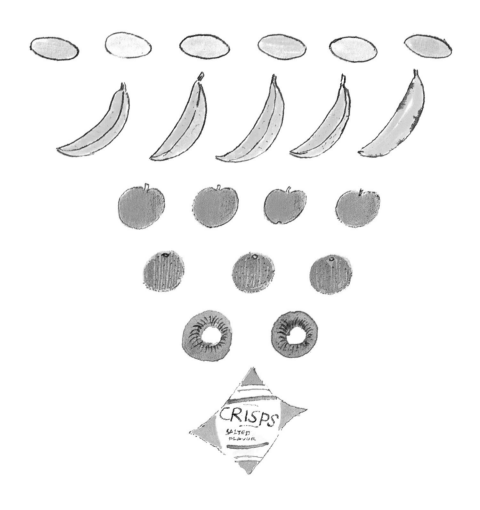

"I want those eggs," said the bear, " and if you don't give them to me I will hug all the breath out of you."

"If I threw an egg up in the air," said Steven, "you are so slow I bet you couldn't even catch it."

"Me slow!" said the bear . . .

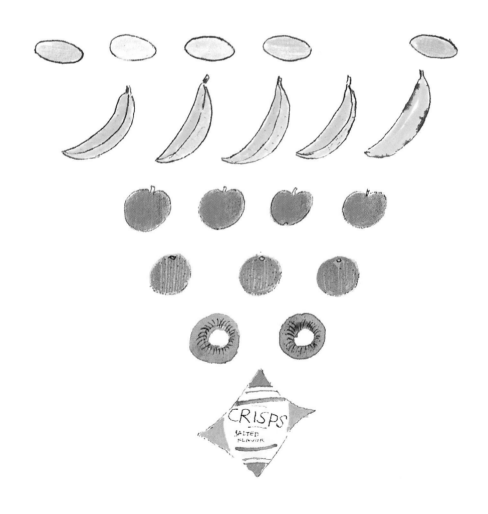

And Steven hurried on home carrying his basket. But when he got to the house where the nasty dog lived there was a monkey.

"Give me those bananas," said the monkey, "or I'll pull your hair."

"If I threw a banana on to that kennel, you're so noisy I bet you couldn't get it without waking the dog."

"Me noisy!" said the monkey . . .

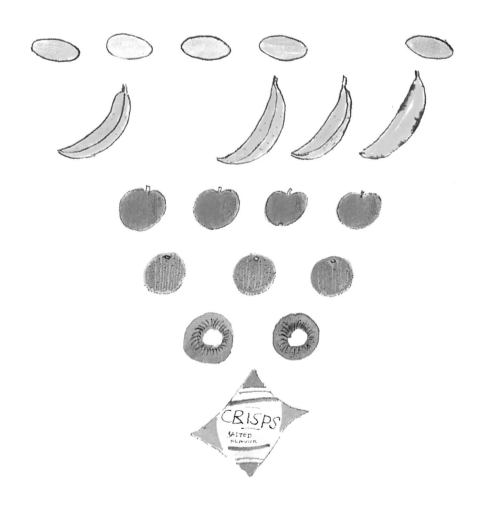

So Steven hurried on home carrying his basket. But when he got to where the men were digging up the pavement there was a kangaroo.

"Give me those apples you have in your basket," said the kangaroo, or I'll thump you."
 "If I threw an apple over that tent, you're so clumsy I bet you couldn't even jump over to get it."
 "Me clumsy!" said the kangaroo . . .

And Steven hurried on home carrying his basket. But when he got to the litter basket there was a goat.

"Give me the oranges you have in your basket," said the goat, "or I'll butt you over the fence."

"If I put an orange in that litter basket, you're so stupid I bet you couldn't even get it out."

"Me stupid!" said the goat . . .

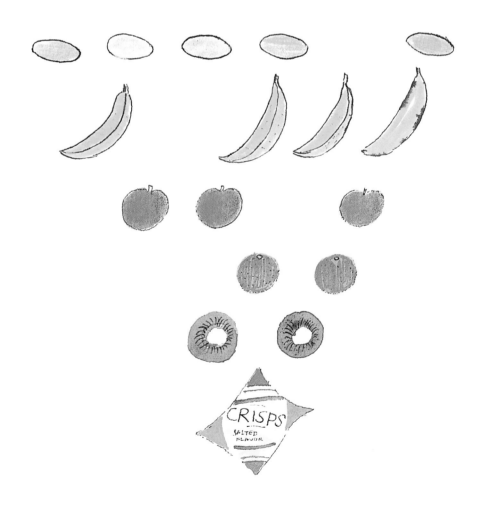

117

So Steven hurried on home carrying his basket.
But when he got to the gap in the railings there was a pig.

"Give me those doughnuts," said the pig, " or I'll squash you against the railings."
"If I put the doughnuts through that gap in the railings, you're so fat I bet you couldn't squeeze through and get them."
"Me fat!" said the pig . . .

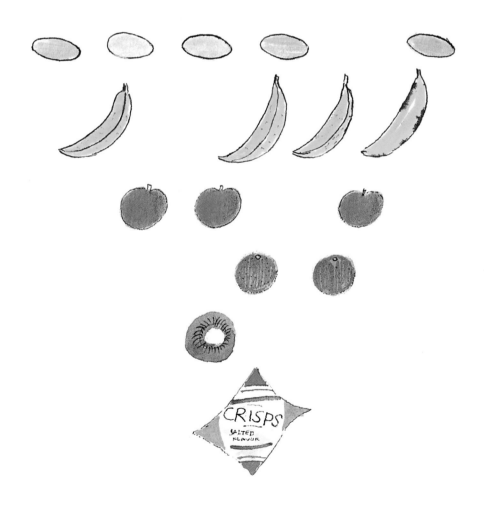

So Steven hurried on home carrying his basket.
  But when he got to number 25 there was
an elephant.

"Give me those crisps," said the elephant, "or I'll whack you with my trunk."

"If I put these crisps through that letter box, your trunk is so short I bet you could not even reach it."

"My trunk short!" said the elephant . . .

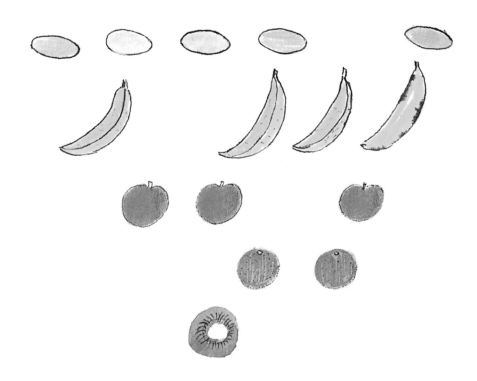

And Steven hurried on home carrying his basket.
   But when he got to his own house, there was
his mother.

"Where on earth have you been, Steven? I only asked you to get six eggs, five bananas, four apples, three oranges, two doughnuts and a packet of crisps. How could it have taken so long?"

Courtney

"We would really like to have a dog," the children said. "Our house would be much better with a dog. The dog would guard the house and it could play with us."

"There are lots of dogs at the Dogs` Home. Can't we please have one?"

"Dogs need feeding and walking."   "And they make a mess everywhere."

"We will walk the dog and feed it."   "And we will clean up the mess."

"Please, can we?"   "Oh, very well then, if you must."

"Make sure it's a proper dog. One with a pedigree.
And remember you'll both have to take care of it."

The children looked at lots of dogs. None of them seemed
to be what they wanted.

"Have you a dog that nobody wants?" they asked the man.
"All the dogs we have seen will find homes easily."
"We do have a dog called Courtney," said the man.
"Nobody wants Courtney."

"We don't know anything about him," said the man. "We don't know where he came from. Nobody wants him and he's an old dog."

"We want Courtney," said the children, and they took him home.

"What on earth have you got there?" said the parents. "Why didn't you get a proper dog? He's old and he's a mongrel, not a pedigree like we said."

"But Courtney's lovely," said the children.

"Well, it's getting late now and you must be going to bed, Courtney will have to sleep in the kitchen."

The next morning the children raced down
to the kitchen to see their new dog but
Courtney was not there.

"We said the dog was no good. These mongrels, you can't rely on them. Why on earth didn't you get a proper dog like we said?"

That afternoon, Courtney came back dragging
a large trunk behind him.

Once in the house, he opened the trunk, put on a chef's hat and apron, and immediately began to cook a delicious meal.

He changed into waiter's clothes and served
the family round the table.

Courtney then played the violin while the family finished the meal.

Out of his trunk, he took some things to juggle with
and entertain the baby.

Sometimes Courtney would meet other dogs in the park.

But most of the time he spent with the family.

One day, the house caught fire and the family were outside waiting for the fire brigade to arrive.

"Where's Courtney?" said one of the children.
"Where's my baby?" shrieked the mother.

Then they saw Courtney climbing down the ladder, holding the baby.

The fire was put out and the house
was soon repaired and the family were
able to carry on living as usual.

One morning they came downstairs and Courtney was not there. The children looked everywhere, but they could not find Courtney or his trunk. "We told you the dog was no good," said the parents. "If they are not thoroughbreds you cannot rely on them."

The children went to the police station. "We've lost our dog. He's quite old, with big eyebrows. He can play the violin, cook wonderful dinners and he juggles to entertain the baby."

"I'll certainly let you know if an old dog with big eyebrows who can play the violin, cook wonderful dinners and juggle to keep the baby amused is handed in," said the policeman.

That summer, the family went to the seaside for their holidays and they took a boat with them.

Every day the children went out in the boat. The boat was always tied to a rock with a long piece of rope so it would not drift out to sea. But on the last day something awful happened . . .

The rope broke.

They lost the oars.

The boat drifted out to sea.

"Somebody help us!"
cried the mother.

The boat drifted almost
out of sight.

Then suddenly there was a tug.

The boat was being pulled
by something.

Toward the shore.

They never did find out who or what it was that had pulled their boat back to shore.

I wonder what it could have been.

Where's Julius?

"For breakfast," said Mrs Troutbeck, "we have scrambled eggs with mushrooms, cornflakes and some orange juice, which I have unfrozen.

Where's Julius?"

Mr Troutbeck called their son Julius and they all sat down to breakfast.

"For lunch today we are having sardines on toast, a roll and butter, tomatoes, and nothing for pudding.

Where's Julius?"

"Julius says he cannot have lunch with us today because he has made a little home in the other room with three chairs, the old curtains and the broom."

So Mr Troutbeck took the tray with the sardines on toast, a roll and butter, tomato and no pudding to the other room where Julius had made his little home out of three chairs, the old curtains and the broom.

166

"I've got the lamb casserole for supper out of the oven and the potatoes in their jackets and broccoli with butter on top and for afterwards there is roly-poly pudding.

Where's Julius?"

"Julius says he cannot have supper with us just at the moment because he is digging a hole in order to get to the other side of the world."

So Mrs Troutbeck took the lamb casserole, the potatoes in their jackets and broccoli with butter on top and the roly-poly pudding for afterwards to where Julius was digging his hole.

"For breakfast there is sausage, bacon and egg, toast and marmalade and also a glass of Three-Flavour Fruit Juice.

Where's Julius?"

"Julius says he cannot have breakfast with us today because he is riding a camel to the top of the tomb of Neffatuteum which is a pyramid near the Nile in Egypt."

So Mr Troutbeck took the tray with the sausage, bacon and egg, toast and marmalade and the glass of Three-Flavour Fruit Juice — and another for the camel — to Egypt where Julius was riding to the top of the pyramid.

"For lunch there is cheese salad with celery and tomato and an orange for pudding if you want it.

Where's Julius?"

"Julius says he cannot have lunch with us at the moment because he is cooling the hippopotamuses in the Lombo Bombo River in Central Africa, with buckets of muddy water."

So Mr Troutbeck took the tray with the cheese salad with celery and tomato and the orange for pudding to Africa where Julius was pouring buckets of muddy water on the hippopotamuses, to keep them cool.

"Here are the grilled chops for supper. There are baby carrots, garden peas and mashed potato to go with them, and an apple crumble for pudding.

Where's Julius?"

"Julius says he can't have supper with us just at the moment because he is throwing snowballs at the wolves from a sledge in which he is crossing the frozen wastes of Novosti Krosky which lies somewhere in Russia where the winters are long."

So Mrs Troutbeck took the tray with the chop, the baby carrots, garden peas and mashed potato and the apple crumble for pudding to Novosti Krosky, which lies somewhere in Russia where Julius was throwing snowballs at the wolves.

182

"For breakfast we are having boiled eggs, toast and marmalade and the Tropical Fruit Juice that you wanted.

Where's Julius?"

"Julius says he cannot have breakfast with us just at the moment because he is watching the sunrise from the top of the Changa Benang mountains somewhere near Tibet."

So Mr Troutbeck
took the tray with the
boiled egg,
toast and marmalade
and the Tropical Fruit
Juice to the top of the
Changa Benang
mountains
somewhere near
Tibet, where Julius
was watching
the sunrise.

For lunch we are having spaghetti bolognese with lettuce and cucumber. For pudding there is plum duff.

Where's Julius?"

"Julius says he can't have lunch with us at the moment because he is on a raft which he has made from pieces of wood and old oil drums and he is about to shoot the rapids on the Chico Neeko River somewhere in Peru in South America."

So Mrs Troutbeck took the tray with the spaghetti bolognese, the lettuce and cucumber and the plum duff to the Chico Neeko River in South America where Julius was about to shoot the rapids on his raft.

190

"For supper today there is Lancashire hot-pot, and steamed pudding for afterwards.

Is Julius building a home out of old curtains, chairs and a broom?

Digging a hole to get to the other side of the world?

Riding a camel up a pyramid?

Cooling the hippos that stand in the Lombo Bombo River?

Throwing snowballs at wolves in Novosti Krosky where the winters are long?

Is he climbing the Changa Benang mountains, or shooting the rapids on the Chico Neeko River in South America?

Perhaps he is helping the young owls to learn to fly in the trees at the end of the road or tucking the polar bears in their beds somewhere in Antarctica?"

"Betty," said Mr Troutbeck, "tonight Julius is having supper at home."